Rub the stickers to release the delicious scent!

Shopkins™

Once you shop...You can't stop!

A SANTA SURPRISE!

SIZZLE PRESS

Christmas was coming and the Shopkins were very excited. Apple Blossom was in charge of decorating all the shops in Shopville, so she gathered everyone together and promised to find a job for them all.

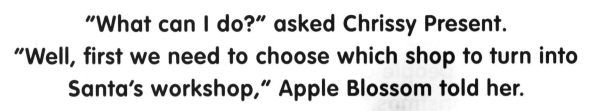

"What can I do?" asked Chrissy Present.
"Well, first we need to choose which **shop** to turn into
Santa's workshop," Apple Blossom told her.

They all agreed the ice cream shop would be the perfect place for Santa's workshop. It was even nice and cold! "And people don't buy much ice cream at Christmas," giggled Poppy Cracker.

"How can I help?" asked Chrissy Present.

"Your job comes later!" Apple Blossom said smiling. She couldn't wait to get started.

"We need to let everyone know that the ice cream shop is now called Santa's workshop," Apple Blossom told them.

SANTA'S WORKSHOP

"That's a job for me!" called Lippy Lips. In her very best handwriting, she wrote SANTA'S WORKSHOP in great big red letters on the window. "Perfect!" all the others cheered.

"Next we need to show that Santa's workshop is in a snowy forest," said Apple Blossom. "I wonder what we can use for the snow."

"What about lots of white frosting?" said Patty Cake, who was topped with lots of white frosting herself. "Or lots of icing sugar?" said Macca Roon, who was dusted with icing sugar.

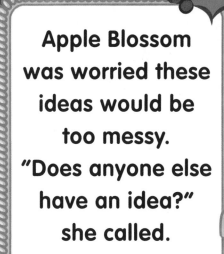

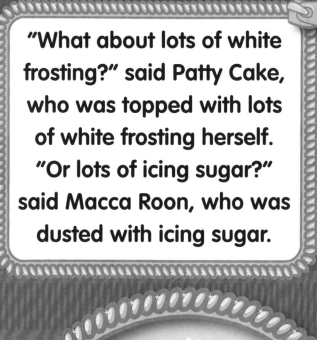

Apple Blossom was worried these ideas would be too messy. "Does anyone else have an idea?" she called.

"Perhaps," said Sammy Santa Hat quietly, "we could use lots of white fur blankets?"
"That's brilliant!" said Apple Blossom. Everyone helped lay white fur blankets by the entrance of the shop.

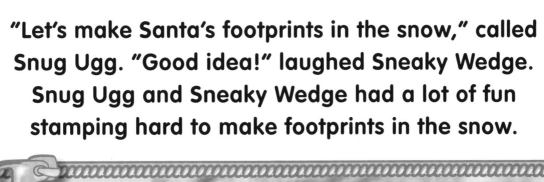

"Let's make Santa's footprints in the snow," called Snug Ugg. "Good idea!" laughed Sneaky Wedge. Snug Ugg and Sneaky Wedge had a lot of fun stamping hard to make footprints in the snow.

"The snow looks great," cried Apple Blossom, "but how are we going to show that Santa's workshop is in the middle of a deep forest?"

"That's where I can help," called Teresa Tree as she stood in the middle of all the white blankets.

"I know I'm only one tree," Teresa continued, "but if I stand tall and spread out my branches, it will look as if there are lots of trees!" She was right! "Fantastic!" chuckled Apple Blossom. "It looks just like a real snowy forest," cried Holly Wreath.

Their next job was to decorate Santa's workshop. "Let's start with the outside," said Apple Blossom. She scratched her head, wondering exactly what the workshop should look like. She had no idea!

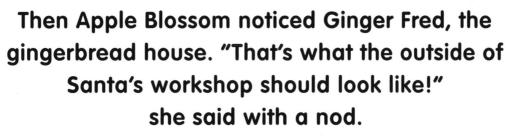

Then Apple Blossom noticed Ginger Fred, the gingerbread house. "That's what the outside of Santa's workshop should look like!" she said with a nod.

The Shopkins had a great time decorating the outside of the shop. They sang carols as they painted the door and windows.

"The front of the shop looks just as pretty as Ginger Fred now," said Holly Wreath as she jumped onto the door. "Except it's a lot bigger," chuckled Chrissy Present.

It was now time to decorate the inside.
"Santa's workshop would probably have lots of little
tables for all his presents," said Wild Carrot.
"What can we use?"

Ornament Annie noticed some old cardboard boxes stacked up in the corner. "How about these?" she asked eagerly. "All we have to do is cover them with pretty paper."

Apple Blossom looked around, wondering what else would be inside Santa's workshop. "We need a cozy log fire!" she cried. So, the Shopkins quickly made a pretend fire, using old cardboard rolls for the logs and crinkly yellow and red wrapping paper for the flames.

"I'll sit on a chair next to the fire," said Sammy Santa Hat. "It will look as if Santa left his hat there to keep it warm."

"You always pick the easiest jobs, Sammy!" Patty Cake laughed.

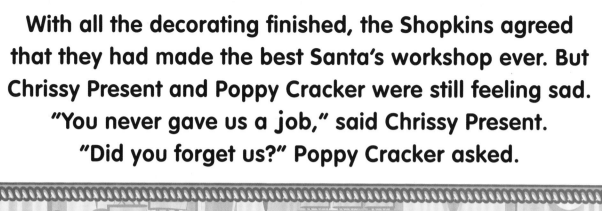

With all the decorating finished, the Shopkins agreed that they had made the best Santa's workshop ever. But Chrissy Present and Poppy Cracker were still feeling sad. "You never gave us a job," said Chrissy Present. "Did you forget us?" Poppy Cracker asked.

"Not at all," chuckled Apple Blossom. "You two have the most important job. You are to be some of the presents in Santa's sack."

Chrissy Present and Poppy Cracker beamed happily.

"Apple Blossom was right," grinned Chrissy Present. "We have the best job of all!"

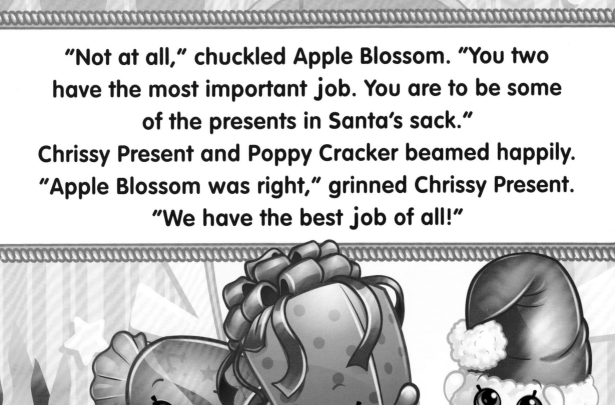